P9-CWD-909

Dragon Scales
AND
Willow Leaves

TERRYL GIVENS

ILLUSTRATED BY

ANDREW PORTWOOD

G. P. PUTNAM'S SONS   NEW YORK

To my children, Nathaniel, Jonathan, Rebecca,
Rachael, Elisabeth, and Andrew
–T. G.

For my girls,
Lauren, Emily, and Deirdre
– with love always
–A. P.

Library of Congress Cataloging-in-Publication Data
Givens, Terryl.   Dragon scales and willow leaves / by Terryl Givens; illustrated by Andrew Portwood   p.   cm.
Summary: Although they are twins, Jonathan and Rachel neither look the same, nor do they see things the same way—especially in the forest.
[1. Individuality–Fiction.   2. Imagination–Fiction.   3. Twins–Fiction.   4. Brothers and sisters–Fiction.]   I. Portwood, Andrew, ill.   II. Title.
PZ7.G458Dr   1997   93-665 CIP AC [E]–dc20 ISBN 0-399-22619-2

1   3   5   7   9   10   8   6   4   2

First Impression

Jonathan and Rachel were twins. But they didn't look the same. And they didn't see things the same way, either.

One day Jonathan went into the woods to hunt
for buried treasure, and Rachel went to look
for robins' nests.

No sooner had they entered the forest than shadows
fell around them. Ahead, in a clearing, they saw
a flicker of red and heard a stirring, rustling . . .

"DRAGON!" cried Jonathan, and out flew his
sword. It slashed through the air, striking and
stabbing until the air was full of fluttering
dragon scales.

Rachel didn't see any dragon. She was watching
the leaves of a weeping willow float softly down,
making a colored carpet that shimmered
and rustled in the breeze.

Jonathan charged on ahead while Rachel stopped
to pick a forget-me-not.

The path beyond was quiet, until the still
was broken by shrieks and howls from treetops
high above. "Ambush!" yelled Jonathan.
"We're being attacked by...

"FOREST TROLLS!" From every branch of every tree they threw rocks and spears and waved their clubs. But Jonathan's shield was like a wall and his sword like an angry bee, and they escaped unharmed. "We're safe now, Rachel," he whispered.

Rachel was smiling at some quarreling blue jays
and frisky squirrels, who shook loose some
pine needles and an occasional acorn.

Coming out of the dark forest, they took a shortcut
across a rushing stream.

But when they heard sloshing and slapping,
they turned to face a...

"PIRATE SHIP!" shouted Jonathan. And at once
the ground shuddered with the roar of cannons,
and the bursting bombs showered them with spray.

Rachel didn't see any pirates. She had discovered
some boisterous bullfrogs, splashing their noisy way
from rock to rock.

By now Jonathan knew they had better make a run
for home.

But when they reached the hilltop, hundreds
and thousands of tall figures with golden hair
and suits of green blocked their way....

"VIKINGS!" gasped Jonathan. "Send me the mightiest of your warriors," he shouted. "I am not afraid!"
The Vikings were so stunned that they froze in terror, while he and Rachel passed safely through.

Rachel wondered how the Vikings managed
to hide so well among the countless rows of corn,
with their ripe ears and golden tassels bending
and nodding in the breeze.

With his castle now in view, Jonathan ran to meet
the three knights, who bowed and ushered him
into the presence of the queen.

Rachel didn't notice the knights or the queen.
She was too happy to be home again.

And just in time for supper.